1/12

The Mysterious & Unknown

Urban Legends

by Gail B. Stewart

ReferencePoint Press®

San Diego, CA

©2012 ReferencePoint Press, Inc.
Printed in the United States

For more information, contact:
ReferencePoint Press, Inc.
PO Box 27779
San Diego, CA 92198
www.ReferencePointPress.com

LIBRARY OF CONGRESS CATALOGING-IN-PUBLICATION DATA

Stewart, Gail B. (Gail Barbara), 1949-
  Urban legends / by Gail B. Stewart.
    p. cm. -- (Mysterious & unknown)
  Includes bibliographical references and index.
  ISBN-13: 978-1-60152-185-9 (hardback)
  ISBN-10: 1-60152-185-5 (hardback)
  1. Urban folklore--Juvenile literature. I. Title.
GR78.S84 2012
398.2--dc22   2011003910

CONTENTS

FOREWORD

"Strange is our situation here upon earth."
—*Albert Einstein*

Since the beginning of recorded history, people have been perplexed, fascinated, and even terrified by events that defy explanation. While science has demystified many of these events, such as volcanic eruptions and lunar eclipses, some remain outside the scope of the provable. Do UFOs exist? Are people abducted by aliens? Can some people see into the future? These questions and many more continue to puzzle, intrigue, and confound despite the enormous advances of modern science and technology.

It is these questions, phenomena, and oddities that Reference-Point Press's *The Mysterious & Unknown* series is committed to exploring. Each volume examines historical and anecdotal evidence as well as the most recent theories surrounding the topic in debate. Fascinating primary source quotes from scientists, experts, and eyewitnesses as well as in-depth sidebars further inform the text. Full-color illustrations and photos add to each book's visual appeal. Finally, source notes, a bibliography, and a thorough index provide further reference and research support. Whether for research or the curious reader, *The Mysterious & Unknown* series is certain to satisfy those fascinated by the unexplained.

INTRODUCTION

What Is an Urban Legend?

Maggie Schuler is 23, but she remembers hearing the horrible story in high school as if it happened yesterday. "I was in 11th grade," she says. "Our geometry class had finished up our work early, and Mr. Jessup, our teacher, was just talking to us about stuff—he was really nice that way—he would just talk about things in the news, stuff that was interesting or unusual. That particular day, he told us this story about something that happened to a guy named Dan, a cousin of his college roommate. And seriously, for years that story completely changed the way I thought about traveling."[1]

A Ring of Organ Thieves

According to Jessup, Dan was a computer systems analyst, and he had gone to Las Vegas, Nevada, on business. He was not a big gambler, so he was not interested in spending time in the casinos. However, on the last night of his trip, he strolled through one of

the biggest casinos and treated himself to a drink at the bar. While he was sitting there watching the activity around him, a beautiful woman smiled at him. When he smiled back at her, she walked over and they had a conversation. After a while she invited him to her room for a drink.

Dan accepted, and when they got to her hotel room, she poured him a glass of wine. He took a sip, and that was the last thing he remembered. Hours later he woke up, inexplicably sitting in a bathtub filled with ice water. Feeling confused, sluggish, and oddly disconnected from his body, Dan noticed that next to the tub were a phone and a note that read, "Don't move. Call the front desk and tell them to call 911. Tell them you're in room 776."[2]

Frightened, Dan made the call, and within a few minutes an ambulance arrived. The emergency medical technicians noticed what appeared to be a fresh surgical scar on Dan's back. When he arrived at the hospital, doctors confirmed that one of Dan's kidneys had been removed. One of the doctors told Dan that he was not the first victim of organ thieves; there had been a ring of them operating in the Las Vegas area.

A black market had sprung up, with disreputable people cashing in on the demand for kidneys to be transplanted into people whose kidneys had failed. The scenario was always the same—a woman would befriend a man who was in the city alone, and after inviting him to her room, would slip a powerful drug into his drink, which would render him unconscious for several hours. Once he was unconscious, two people who had medical experience (doctors or medical students, most likely) removed one of his kidneys, sewed him back up, and left him in the cold bath to keep the bleeding and swelling to a minimum until he awoke and called for help.

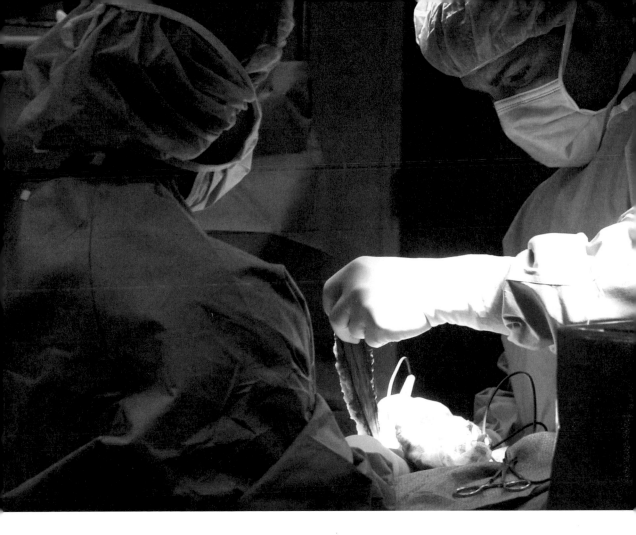

A Strangely Familiar Story

Schuler and her classmates were horrified by their teacher's story. Believing it to be true, they told others, who likely repeated it to their own friends and relatives. Schuler remembers:

> Nobody could stop talking about it. It was a big deal—we told our parents and everybody we knew. Most people were like me, completely grossed out by something like that. But I do remember that my parents were kind of skeptical, which made me mad. I said, "Really, how can you think my teacher

Urban legends
spread farther and
faster over the
Internet than by any
other means.

would make something like that up! I mean, he and Dan's cousin were roommates!"[3]

What was so strange, Schuler says, is that two years later, when she was in college, she heard the same story, but with several variations. She says:

I actually had this discussion one night with a bunch of friends. One guy says he'd heard the same story, only it happened to a tourist in India. Someone else heard it happened in Miami Beach, only it was a woman who'd been the target, not a man. Another one happened in New Orleans. At that point, I realized my parents had been right—the whole thing was just a made-up story. Made me feel really dumb.[4]

Contemporary Myths

Stories like this one are known as urban legends—and there are hundreds of thousands of them. Urban legends seem to the listener as if they could be true, although most are not. Many of the people who pass on urban legends believe them to be true as they tell them. Because the stories are horrifying, scary, or funny, they are immensely popular. And whereas centuries ago they spread by word of mouth or in letters, in the twenty-first century urban legends often speed along the Internet, reaching around the world in a matter of minutes.

The term *urban legends* is misleading, for these stories do not necessarily take place in cities. The term is merely a way to distinguish the stories from the myths, fables, and legends that arose centuries ago, before the explosion of big cities and suburbs. In fact, many people who study these stories use another term. They call them contemporary myths.

In ancient times people told stories about gods and goddesses, frightening monsters, and ordinary people who sometimes accomplished extraordinary feats. These stories were told and retold, passed from one listener to another and from generation to generation. Along the way details were changed or added, as is the case in oral traditions. A new character might be added or the description of a monster embellished to make a story scarier, funnier, or more compelling.

Everyone Loves a Good Story

The content of modern urban legends also differs significantly from stories passed along from earlier times in that it reflects the ideas, values, and worries that constitute modern life. One such modern story might be about a well-known movie star dying in a horrible accident or about a woman who discovers a severed finger in a bowl of chili at a fast-food restaurant. Still another might be a more pleasant tale—a man who stops to help a stranger change a flat tire and is dumbfounded when he is rewarded with a million dollars.

Though the subject matter and settings of urban legends differ from older legends, they share an important attribute: They are enthusiastically told and retold again and again. Says Marlys Olson, a lifelong student of folklore traditions: "We cannot, no matter how much we resist, stop ourselves from passing along a good story—which is what an urban legend is. It's in our nature, maybe in our DNA. We are inveterate listeners as well as tellers. And whether the 'absolutely true' part of the story is *not* really true, it seems to make no difference for our appetite for them."[5]

CHAPTER 1

"Too Good to Be True"

Folklorists and others who study urban legends say that while these stories differ widely in subject matter, most urban legends share some common characteristics. The most important of these is their relationship with the truth. According to Jan Harold Brunvand, a renowned urban legend expert, "Urban legends are true stories that are too good to be true."[6]

In other words, an urban legend claims to be true, but as the story unfolds—usually with a shocking, funny, ironic, or scary ending—it goes just a step too far to be completely believable to the listener. *Completely* is the operative word, for the best urban legends are impossible for the listener simply to dismiss out of hand as being untrue. The story may seem far-fetched, but the best urban legends have a quality that makes the listener feel that there is at least a possibility of truth.

And that, says Brunvand, is astonishing, considering the topics covered in popular urban legends:

> [In urban legends] people do things like fill cars with cement, microwave their pets, get bitten by poisonous snakes concealed in imported garments, lose their grandmother's corpse from the car roof, buy a Porsche for a mere $50, mistake a rat for a stray Chihuahua, sit on an exploding toilet, steal a package that contains only a dead cat . . . just to mention a few typical plots. All of these things could conceivably happen, but it is thoroughly unlikely that they really did happen in all the different times and places that the legend-tellers describe.[7]

Credibility Is in the Details

So what is it that prevents listeners from rolling their eyes and saying, "No way"? One of the most important ways by which an urban legend gains credibility is in the way it is told. As Maggie Schuler and her fellow students found, the story about the kidney transplant was believable because of how the information was presented.

"Seriously," she says, "when I look back on that time, if Mr. Jessup had just said something like, 'You know, some criminals are drugging people, stealing their kidneys and selling them on the black market,' it probably wouldn't have been that interesting. And for sure, it would have sounded just plain phony."[8]

That is one of the most important elements of a good urban legend, say experts. An urban legend is not simply a recitation of alleged facts, but rather a narrative that involves the listener

from the very beginning. In the kidney theft story, the urban legend is grounded in a particular city and involves a particular person who is victimized. Other details make the story more interesting—and therefore, believable—such as the facts that the victim's job was computer analysis and that he had never spent time in Las Vegas before. Further details about the position of the note and phone by the bathtub give the listener a clear image of the setting, too. All of those details help make an admittedly outrageous story into something at least partially believable.

Detail is not the only element of an urban legend that makes it credible. Even more important is the source of the story. Urban legends are unique in that at the very beginning of the story, the teller almost always establishes a certain type of relationship to the protagonist—the person at the center of the story. The teller might say, "This happened to my cousin's neighbor," or, "The son of my mother's dentist actually had this experience." Experts call this the "friend of a friend," or FOAF syndrome. According to urban legend researcher Brandon Toropov, tellers do this deliberately. "In one sense," he says, "they are claiming some connection to the characters in the story; in another sense, they are putting some distance between themselves and the events."[9]

Modern-Day Fables

Another characteristic that many urban legends have in common is that they teach a lesson, or moral, as Aesop's fables from the 600s BC did. In Aesop's "The Tortoise and the Hare," for example, listeners heard the improbable story of a lightning-fast rabbit who challenges a tortoise to a race. Even after giving the tortoise a head start, the rabbit takes a nap because he has absolute confidence that he will win. But while the rabbit sleeps, the tortoise plods on and ultimately wins the race. The moral, according to Aesop, is that it is always more important to work carefully and steadily than to be quick but cocky.

Urban legends that are meant to make such a point never actually declare the lesson; rather, the moral is implied by the events that occur. The story known as "The Lady at the Funeral" is a good example of this. It involves a New Zealand woman named Leslie who is saddened to hear that her aunt has died. Though she did not know her aunt well, she feels she should attend the funeral. Her aunt had instructed that her remains be cremated, so the funeral was to be held at a crematorium.

When Leslie arrives at the crematorium, she finds four separate chapels and takes a seat in the first one just as the funeral is beginning. After a few moments, however, she realizes that she has chosen the wrong chapel. Because she feels embarrassed by her mistake and worried that her sudden departure will disrupt the proceedings, she stays until the service ends. At that point she signs the guest book along with all of the other mourners.

Several weeks later she is stunned to receive a check for several thousand pounds (more than $4,000) from a lawyer. It seems that the man whose funeral she mistakenly attended had stipulated in his will that his estate be divided equally among every person who attended his funeral.

Though there has never been a documented case of money being inherited in this way in New Zealand or anywhere else, the story has spread throughout the world. The implied moral of the story is that thoughtfulness—in this case not wanting to disrupt a funeral in progress—can be rewarded in a big way.

Irresistible Irony

Another element of some of the most widely circulated urban legends is irony, the odd twist at the ending that is the opposite of what the listener might expect. Teacher Berneeta Jacques says, "I always explain irony to my students as that ingredient in a story that makes the listeners' eyes get really wide, and they say, 'You're *kidding!* Seriously?'"[10]

One such legend involves Charles Drew, a twentieth-century African American physician and medical researcher. In addition to his work in perfecting methods of blood transfusions, he also developed techniques that allowed doctors to store blood—leading to the establishment of blood banks in the early years of World War II. In addition, he fought against the practice of keeping separate blood banks for blacks and whites.

These details of Drew's life and work are all true; however, his death has become the subject of an urban legend. That story begins on April 1, 1950, when Drew and three other doctors were driving from Washington, DC, to a clinic in Tuskegee, Alabama. The doctors took turns driving throughout the night, and during Drew's shift he fell asleep. The car went off the road on a North Carolina roadway, injuring all of them—but Drew most severely.

They were taken to the nearest hospital emergency room, where doctors realized that Drew needed a blood transfusion to save his life. However, because he was black, and because the South still segregated blacks, the hospital denied him care, allowing Drew to bleed to death in the hospital hallway. The story was bitterly ironic—a man who had devoted his life to making blood transfusions easier and safer was denied that very lifesaving procedure because of his race.

Soldiers organize blood bank containers during World War II. The work of the African American physician and medical researcher Charles Drew made it possible to store blood and led to the establishment of blood banks. The circumstances of Drew's death became the subject of an urban legend.

Not the Way It Happened

The problem with this hospital story, which has circulated widely for many years, is that it never happened. The true part of the story is that Drew died from injuries sustained in an automobile accident while driving with colleagues to an Alabama clinic. However, he was admitted without hesitation to the hospital, where doctors discovered that his injuries were so serious that they were unable to save him. According to one of Drew's colleagues (also African American) who was also injured in the accident, "We all received the very best of care. The doctors started treating us immediately . . . [but] even the most heroic efforts couldn't have saved him."[11]

Interestingly, however, the urban legend surrounding Drew's death spread quickly and was reported as fact by several American newspapers and magazines shortly after the accident. As late as the 1970s, the legend was still going strong. In season two of the popular television show *M.A.S.H.*, two American army surgeons told a racist soldier the story of Drew and how he had bled to death because the whites-only hospital refused to give him care. Urban legend experts maintain that the eagerness with which people were willing to embrace the legend highlights the fact that discrimination was widespread at that time, and such a story was very believable—especially to black Americans.

"Us Versus Them"

Even without the irony of the Charles Drew story, a great many urban legends tap into commonly held prejudices or suspicions about other cultures. In fact, such prejudices are so deeply entrenched that it is not surprising these urban legends (sometimes known as "Us Versus Them" legends) spread quickly and ring true to so many listeners.

One such legend, which has been circulating in various forms since the 1960s, can still be heard today. It involves an Iowa couple vacationing in Mexico with their four-year-old daughter. On the last day of their trip, they decide to attend a little carnival. The father puts his little girl on the merry-go-round—something she has never tried before.

At first she enjoys herself immensely; she is thrilled to be riding a green-painted horse—green is her favorite color. But within a few minutes, she begins to complain that the horse is biting her and she wants to get off the ride. Her father assures her that wooden horses cannot bite and says they need to wait to get off until the merry-go-round stops.

But by the time the ride slows to a stop, the father is horrified to discover that his daughter is clearly in distress. She is pale and clammy and is laboring to breathe, and within a few minutes she dies in her father's arms. The horses on the merry-go-round, according to the story, are old and full of cracks—and apparently have become a choice nesting place for poisonous snakes. In this case one snake evidently crawled out and bit the child on the leg.

Though the legend does not actually state the danger of visiting Mexico, the warning is implied. Other versions of this story involve merry-go-round horses imported from India or China— also places that some Americans may feel uneasy about. In one early form of this same story, the carnival takes place in an American city in the Midwest, but the infected horses come from one of the southern states. "This is a nice touch to the story—legendary venomous serpents and other nasty things often originate somewhere in the South," writes Brunvand, "possibly revealing northerners' suspicions of that region."[12]

Not Always Scary

Not all of the "Us Versus Them" legends are scary. Sometimes the point is to poke fun at another group of people. An urban legend from Canada that mocks US arrogance toward Canadians revolves around a conversation between Canadian civil defense authorities and a US ship off the coast of Newfoundland on October 10, 1995. Although this exchange never really occurred, the story has been repeated so often that many believe it to be true. The tale is in the form of a dialogue conducted via radio:

"We were totally horrified—a little penny could be so dangerous."

—A woman remembering hearing that a penny dropped from the Empire State Building could kill someone.

A Presidential Urban Legend

Almost since the day Barack Obama announced his candidacy for the Democratic presidential nomination in 2007, an urban legend concerning his birthplace has swirled around the Internet. Obama was born in Hawaii on August 4, 1961, to an American mother and a Kenyan father—and he has produced a birth certificate (both short and long forms) and a newspaper notice to prove it.

Americans: Please divert your course 15 degrees to the north to avoid a collision.

Canadians: Recommend you divert YOUR course 15 degrees to the south to avoid a collision.

Americans: This is the captain of a U.S. Navy ship. I say again, divert YOUR course.

But according to a well-known urban legend, Obama was not born in the United States. If this were the case, he could not be president, because the US Constitution states that only someone born in the United States is eligible to run for president. Despite Obama's perfectly adequate proof of eligibility to hold the presidency, the urban legend about his birthplace lives on, as urban legends do. The *St. Petersburg Times* website notes that "there is not one shred of evidence to support [the urban legend]. And that's true no matter how many people cling to some hint of doubt and use the Internet to fuel their innate sense of distrust."

Quoted in Amy Hollyfield, "Obama's Birth Certificate: Final Chapter," PolitiFact.com, June 27, 2008. www.politifact.com.

Canadians: No, I say again, you divert YOUR course.

Americans: THIS IS THE AIRCRAFT CARRIER U.S.S. ABRAHAM LINCOLN, THE SECOND LARGEST SHIP IN THE UNITED STATES' ATLANTIC FLEET. WE ARE ACCOMPANIED BY THREE DESTROYERS, THREE CRUISERS AND

Contrary to the
long-standing urban
legend, America's
founders did not
gather to sign the
Declaration of
Independence on
July 4, 1776.

NUMEROUS SUPPORT VEHICLES. I DEMAND THAT YOU CHANGE YOUR COURSE 15 DEGREES NORTH. THAT'S ONE-FIVE DEGREES NORTH, OR COUNTER MEASURES WILL BE UNDERTAKEN TO ENSURE THE SAFETY OF THIS SHIP.

Canadians: This is a lighthouse. Your call.[13]

The Most Famous Signature Ever

Some of the oldest urban legends endure because people are reluctant to give them up; often the legends are far more interesting than the truth. One such legend revolves around John Hancock, who was the first to sign the Declaration of Independence. For generations, American schoolchildren have learned that the founders gathered to sign that famous document on July 4, 1776, and that Hancock signed first—knowing full well that it would be considered a treasonous act against Britain.

According to the story, Hancock made his signature so large—a full 5 inches (12.7cm) across—to encourage his peers to be courageous and also to make a statement to England's monarch, King George III. In one famous account, Hancock is said to have exclaimed as he signed the document: "There! John Bull [a personification of England, much like Uncle Sam for the United States] can read my name without spectacles and may now double his reward of 500 pounds for my head. That is my defiance."[14]

As a result of his brave act, Hancock's signature with the flourish beneath became the most well known of any in American history. An insurance company bearing his name features his signature in gigantic letters at the top of a Boston skyscraper. In fact, his name has become so famous that "put your John Hancock" on something has become synonymous with "sign it." But although the story is dramatic and interesting, it never happened.

Contrary to urban legend, America's founders did not gather on July 4, 1776, to sign the Declaration of Independence. The Congress did ratify it that day, but not until days later, when the document had been written in its finished, revised form, was it signed—and then only by two people: Hancock, as president of the Congress, and Charles Thomson, the secretary. (Other delegates signed it weeks later, after it was printed in its final form.)

With those two signatures, the Declaration of Independence was printed and distributed to each colony's legislature, as well as to the Continental army, where officers read it to their troops. It was not addressed to King George, say historians, so it would have made no sense for Hancock to say anything about the king reading it without his glasses. Neither Thomson nor any other members of Congress ever recorded such a comment in the accounts of the signing. It is a good story, say scholars, but not good history.

The "Did You Know?" Legend

Not all urban legends have detailed story lines. Some, which experts refer to as the "Did You Know?" urban legend, tend to be short on details but still manage to gain wide acceptance. Unlike most urban legends, proving or disproving a "Did You Know?" legend is sometimes only a matter of applying science to see whether or not it is possible.

South Dakotan Clare Pierce, a former elementary school teacher, recalls a story told by her seventh-grade teacher. The teacher, she says,

OPPOSITE:
*According
to one urban
legend, a penny
dropped from
the top of New
York's Empire
State Building
(pictured
center) would
gain so much
velocity that
anyone hit by
it on the street
below would
die instantly.*
**Discovery
Channel's
MythBusters
show disproved
this well-known
story.**

told us that a penny dropped from the top of the Empire State Building would gain so much velocity that it would almost be like a bullet, and could instantly kill a person walking underneath. In fact, she told us someone *had* been killed, a lady doing some shopping. A tourist at the top [of the Empire State Building] had dropped the coin for fun, not realizing it was dangerous, and it embedded itself in her skull. I have a very strong memory of sitting in that classroom, and all of us going, "Yow!" We were totally horrified—a little penny could be so dangerous just dropped randomly from the top of the Empire State Building![15]

To the Discovery Channel's special effects experts Jamie Hyneman and Adam Savage of the show *MythBusters*, this story seemed ripe for testing. Using a variety of experiments and scientific equipment, they boiled the question down to this: "How fast would a penny go if it fell one thousand two hundred and eighty feet [the height of the building], and what kind of damage would it do?"[16]

Hyneman and Savage undertook a series of experiments using a wind tunnel (to replicate the conditions and air currents) and a dummy created with a skull the exact thickness of that of a human being. They learned that because of air drafts, which sometimes even made the penny "float" at times, the fastest a penny could accelerate was 65 miles per hour (104.6kph). With the very small mass of a penny, at that speed it could not even bruise the head of a person walking below. As Savage concluded, "The penny drop myth isn't worth a dime."[17]

Pierce admits that she was torn between emotions when learning that the story was merely an urban legend. "Part of me was glad that it never happened, and that people don't need to worry about getting killed by falling pennies," she says. "But I admit I felt pretty foolish. I've told my own kids, and I'm pretty sure I've mentioned it to most of the fifth grade classes I've taught over the years. So there you go—I guess I've just been keeping an urban legend alive!"[18]

Hazy Origins

The final important characteristic of most urban legends is that they have no known origin. Some folklorists have tried to uncover the origins of specific urban legends—or at least approximate the time when the legends first began—but most of these efforts fail.

The most famous of the urban legend researchers, Brunvand, admits that even the experts are stumped when it comes to finding a story's source. "Frankly, my friends," he writes, "I don't know. After nearly two decades of collecting and studying this vibrant genre of modern folklore I'm still pretty much in the dark about how such tales originate."[19]

One thing experts do know is how rapidly and widely these legends spread. Once a good urban legend gets started, if it is interesting, funny, or horrifying enough, those who love to tell and hear good stories simply cannot spread it fast enough.

CHAPTER 2

Very Scary

A large number of urban legends are meant to scare people. They tap into common human fears such as the fear of becoming the victim of a violent crime, of being alone in the dark, and of becoming infected with a horrible disease. According to Jan Harold Brunvand, urban legends are the scariest of the scary stories, just by their very nature:

> Urban legends . . . are scary when they combine horror fiction with the details of real life. In typical ULs [urban legends] you encounter shocks such as lurking criminals, threatening maniacs, vague unknown dangers, faulty products, and isolated victims, all set in the context of everyday life. Such stories are told by a friend as something that happened to his or her close friend (a friend of a friend . . .). Urban legends are packed with local details and related with an air of conviction.[20]

Alone at Night

One of the most well-known of these scary urban legends has been around in various forms since the late 1950s, although it is not clear whether it has any basis in fact. Like many of the best urban legends, its details have evolved to make it as frightening in the twenty-first century as it was originally. The story rotates around Ginny, a 13-year-old girl from a Chicago suburb who is babysitting three little boys. Ginny had been babysitting since she was 11 and prided herself on being responsible and reliable.

On this particular night she puts the boys to bed and is just turning on the television in the living room when she hears an odd noise. Quickly turning down the volume, she listens again, but hears nothing. Just to be safe, she makes sure the doors are all securely locked and then tries to relax by watching TV. The phone rings soon after she turns the television on, and she is startled to hear a raspy voice asking if she has checked on the children. Certain it was a prank call, she hangs up and resumes watching her show. After a few minutes, the phone rings a second time, and again the same raspy voice tells her to check on the boys. This time, he calls her by name—which really frightens her. She calls her mother, who instructs her to call the police, which she does.

Ginny is unable to tell the 911 dispatcher what number the calls are coming from because she does not have caller ID on her phone. She is transferred to a police officer, who tells her to hang up and they will trace the origin of the calls. Moments later the officer phones to say that the calls are coming from a second line in the home—a business phone in an upstairs bedroom. The police, says the officer, are on their way.

When the police arrive, they find all three of the boys upstairs —dead. (The urban legends vary as to the method by which the children died—some versions say the boys were smothered, others say their throats were slashed.) Most versions say that the killer escaped via the second-story window and was never found.

"Flash and Die"

Some of the scariest nighttime urban legends take place in automobiles. One that has been circulating since the mid-1990s issues a warning to California motorists driving at night. According to the story, the Bloods gang is initiating new members in a violent new way. Any prospective member can be "jumped in" to the gang only if he proves that he has the stomach to kill an innocent driver.

According to this urban legend, the gang initiate drives around at night with his headlights turned off. According to one warning distributed via e-mail in November 2010, the initiate "drives along with no headlights on, and the 1st car to flash their headlights at them is now his 'target.' He is now required to turn around and chase that car, then shoot and kill [the] individual in the vehicle."[21]

When this and similar e-mails first began circulating (supposedly by an unnamed police officer in Houston, Texas), experts quickly dispelled this story as an urban legend. John Moore, senior research associate at the National Youth Gang Center, stated that to the best of his knowledge, the "Lights Out" legend is completely false: "I know of no incident in the country where this type of thing occurred," he told a reporter for the *Washington Post*. "This is one of the wonders of the Internet, that you can take something that has no basis in fact and make people believe it."[22]

An Urban Legend Goes Global

Members of the
Bloods gang
show their
colors. One
urban legend,
which gang
experts refute,
involves the
shooting of
unsuspecting
drivers in
California as
part of a Bloods'
initiation rite.
One Canadian
official,
convinced of
the danger to
motorists, sent
a warning to
members of
Parliament.

As with many of the scariest urban legends, this one (usually referred to as "Flash and Die" or "Lights Out!") became global soon after it first appeared—though the gang in the story had changed. In November 1998 the Canadian minister of defense, Art Eggleton, sent an urgent warning to members of the parliament telling them that Canadian gangs were killing motorists in the same way. Later, after learning that the story was only an urban legend, Eggleton informed the parliament that the story was untrue.

But it continued in various forms. In London the story evolved into a warning for ambulance drivers to beware of blinking their lights at oncoming cars that might be driven by gang members. According to a 2004 e-mail warning, the attacks involved "some street gangs in London (particularly South London at present, but it is sure to spread.)"[23]

The London Ambulance Service later issued an update, explaining that the e-mail was a mistake: "The message originated from outside the Service and was forwarded by a member of staff to friends in good faith. Please be assured, however, that we have checked with the Metropolitan Police Service and the information contained within it is not genuine, so the message can be safely deleted."[24]

Death by Needle

In addition to playing on fears of being alone at night or of becoming a victim of violent crime, some urban legends capitalize on the fear of becoming infected with a life-threatening disease and sometimes even vilify those who have the disease. For example, one very popular urban legend began in the 1980s when HIV and AIDS first became known in the United States.

As with many urban legends, the story varies—but in many versions the victim is a young woman arriving late to a movie. As she sits down and slips her coat off, she feels something prick her arm. She realizes, to her horror, that she has a long needle dangling from the back of her arm. Taped to the needle is a note that reads, "You have just been infected with HIV."[25]

According to the story, the astonished woman rushes to the nearest emergency room, the suspicious needle and note in her purse. Doctors speculate that it is a sick joke meant to frighten an innocent moviegoer and that the needle is likely harmless. After more than two hours of tests and other lab work, however, doctors inform the woman that the needle is in fact contaminated with HIV, the virus that causes AIDS. Blood tests later confirm that she has been infected with the virus. According to this urban legend, she died eight months later.

Although the end of the story is usually the same—a fatal diagnosis—the circumstances vary from story to story. Sometimes it is a child who is stuck by a needle when putting his or her hand in a coin return on a pay phone or a candy machine on

the outside chance there would be money there. Sometimes it is someone pricking themselves on the dreaded needle while grabbing the self-serve pump at a gas station. But no matter who the victim is, the "moral" of the story is essentially the same—not only is AIDS dangerous, but people who have the disease are out to infect innocent victims.

The Poisoned Dress

Fear of illness and death plays into a legend that began in the 1940s, but folklorists say it continues to show up in a recycled fashion every few years. The principal characters in one early version of this urban legend are a just-married young couple in a small town in Virginia. Directly after the ceremony, the wedding party and guests go to the local Kiwanis Club for an evening of dinner and dancing.

Everything is going well, except for an odd odor that seems to be coming from the bride's wedding gown. However, as N.E. Genge notes in her book *Urban Legends: The As-Complete-As-One-Could-Be Guide to Modern Myths*, the bride and groom are not worried at first. "Dismissing it as the remnant of dry-cleaning solution being activated by her rising body heat, the bride in her antique dress steps outside with her groom for a few minutes to air out the numerous folds."[26]

But the bride begins to feel dizzy and sick. Worried that something more serious is going on, the groom leaves her outside and runs in to find his uncle, a doctor. Astonishingly, by the time the two men get back outside, the bride is dead. Soon afterward, the medical examiner does an autopsy to try to discover the cause of the seemingly healthy young woman's death. At first he, too, is stumped. But then the grieving widower recalls the odd odor coming from the wedding gown—and an inspection of the dress provides the horrible answer, according to Genge:

> Careful backtracking revealed that the odor came from formaldehyde [a poison once used by morticians to embalm dead bodies] and to the discovery of the local mortician's interesting sideline as a purveyor of expensive period clothing! The mortician, to save on overhead, simply "recycled" the clothes that would otherwise have been buried with clients who had no further use for them![27]

According to this urban legend, the bride's pores opened as she was dancing (the body's natural response to getting warmer), and the formaldehyde got warmer, too. As she danced, the fumes from the cloth entered her body and spread through her system, quickly poisoning her.

Watch Out for the Cleaning Lady!

Some urban legends feed off the fear many people have of hospitals. According to this urban legend from Cape Town, South Africa, hospitals can be fraught with unexpected dangers. In a certain hospital there, doctors, nurses, and administrators have been baffled by an odd coincidence. Every Friday morning nurses find a dead patient in a postsurgical ward—but always in the same bed. The cause of death cannot be discerned, and even checking the air-conditioning and heating ducts for bacteria has yielded no clues.

According to the Internet rumor, after months of patients dying from inexplicable causes, a spokeswoman for Pelonomi

Nostradamus and 9/11

Within days of the 9/11 attacks, urban legends began popping up on the Internet. One of the eeriest was the Internet posting of an alleged prophecy of the event by the sixteenth-century French seer Nostradamus. According to urban legend expert David Emery, very few of the words appearing in this supposed prophecy were actually written by Nostradamus, and those that were have been taken out of context, rearranged, and supplemented with made-up lines. According to Emery, "Not even Nostradamus would want to take credit for this 'prediction,'" which reads like this:

Hospital holds a press conference at which she is able to provide an explanation:

> Further inquiries have now revealed the cause of these deaths. It seems that every Friday morning, a cleaner would enter the ward, remove the plug

In the year of the new century and nine months,
From the sky will come a great King of Terror. . .
The sky will burn at forty-five degrees.
Fire approaches the great new city. . .

In the city of york there will be a great collapse,
2 twin brothers torn apart by chaos
while the fortress falls the great leader will succumb
third big war will begin when the big city is burning.

David Emery, "Did Nostradamus Predict the 9/11 Attacks?," About.com, September 12, 2001. http://urbanlegends.about.com. Quoted in Emery, "Did Nostradamus Predict the 9/11 Attacks?"

that powered the patient's life support system, plug her floor polisher into the vacant socket, and then go about her business. When she had finished her chores, she would plug the life support machine back in and leave, unaware that the patient was now dead. She could not, after all, hear the

screams and eventual death rattle over the whirring of her polisher.[28]

This fictitious news release was included in an e-mail message that began circulating in the late 1990s. According to urban legend researcher Brandon Toropov, it is "a carefully concocted chunk of baloney."[29] Not only does the fabricated story prey on readers' fear of hospitals but also implies a "moral"—in this case that cleaners, janitors, and others who provide menial services are neither intelligent nor safe to employ in hospitals.

The Disgusting Envelopes

The idea that the commonplace activities of daily life could have dire—or at the very least, disgusting—consequences feeds into the urban legend phenomenon. In one story a young woman named Grace is planning a New Year's Eve party. She has planned everything down to the last detail and is happily sending out invitations to more than 100 friends, relatives, and business acquaintances. On this particular day, as she licks one of the envelopes, she gets a small paper cut on her tongue. It bleeds only slightly, and she forgets about it.

A few days later, however, Grace wakes up feeling a little feverish, and her tongue is swollen and very sore. She goes to a doctor, who sees she has what appears be a cyst on her tongue, so he prepares her for minor surgery to remove it. When he cuts into the cyst, however, he is shocked and nauseated. A full-grown cockroach emerges from the cyst. Evidently, there were roach eggs in the envelope glue, and when she cut her tongue, the warm saliva in her mouth acted as the perfect incubator to the eggs—one of which actually hatched.

Though there is no evidence that such an incident ever happened, the legend has been told so often and in so many ways that people swear it has happened to someone they know. According to urban legends researcher David Emery, the story is creepy because it is based on one undeniable fact:

> It's not as if wayward insects never, ever find their way into crevices of the human body—they sometimes do, to the horror not only of the victim but of anyone who happens to hear the tale. But the bulk of infestation legends are just that: legends. They are concocted out of the teeniest, tiniest grains of truth, a generous sprinkling of latent dread, and a heaping helping of imagination. It's hard to resist sharing them with the ones you love.[30]

The Terrorism Connection

Some of the eeriest urban legends rise from a particularly stressful time in society, such as a war or a natural disaster. In the United States few events in recent history have been as frightening as the attacks on the World Trade Center and the Pentagon on September 11, 2001. Within a few weeks of 9/11, people around the world were sharing stories about the attacks, the circumstances of the victims, and even the terrorists themselves. Though a few were verifiable, most were urban legends that seemed designed to evoke in the listeners or e-mail readers rage, fear, and a sense of unease.

One of the most common of the 9/11 urban legends is what folklorists call "The Friendly Terrorist." As with all urban legends, the details vary widely, but in one, a young teacher named Sophia Owens is standing in line in a convenience store in Manhattan on

"[Urban legends] are concocted out of the teeniest, tiniest grains of truth, a generous sprinkling of latent dread, and a heaping helping of imagination."

—Expert David Emery on the scariest urban legends.

The 9/11 terrorist attack on the World Trade Center's Twin Towers, shown here engulfed in flames and smoke, generated an urban legend known as "The Friendly Terrorist." A variation of the same story began circulating after the London transit bombings of 2005.

the Saturday before the 9/11 attacks. She notices that the man ahead of her is paying for a few grocery items, but the cashier is explaining to him that he is 75 cents short. Since he has no more money and seems resigned to leaving one of his purchases behind, Owens volunteers to give him the needed 75 cents.

The man thanks her in somewhat broken English, and as she begins walking to a nearby coffee shop to meet a friend, he calls to her. When she stops, he walks over and quietly warns her not to plan an airplane journey on September 11. It is not until the first plane crashes into the North Tower at 8:46 a.m. on that day that she thinks of the warning and shudders. She is even more frightened when, days into the investigation of the terrorist act, CNN begins to show photos of the al Qaeda terrorists responsible for the attacks—and she recognizes the man she had helped at the convenience store as one of them.

Interestingly, versions of this urban legend also surfaced after the London transit bombings in July 2005. It was then that suicide bombers coordinated a series of explosions on four separate trains, killing 52 commuters and injuring 700. In the days afterward, stories surfaced of kindnesses done to a Middle Eastern shopper who comes up short when paying for groceries or gas. In return the man tells the Good Samaritan (in every story, a woman) to avoid the Tube (the British term for the underground trains) the following day. When the BBC broadcasts photos of the suspected London terrorists, the woman is dumbstruck, for one of them is the man she helped.

A Visual Urban Legend

Some of the most memorable 9/11 urban legends are those paired with photographs. One that began circulating on the Internet two weeks after the attacks shows an unsuspecting tourist standing atop the North Tower. The young man, wearing sunglasses and carrying a backpack, poses for the camera, not realizing that behind him is the first hijacked plane, just a second or two before it crashes into the very tower on which he stands.

Did You Know?

The photo of a tourist atop the World Trade Center on September 11, 2001, is a hoax.

Many people around the world received the photo and then forwarded it to their friends, who then forwarded it to others. In the e-mail accompanying the photo, one sender wrote: "We've seen thousands of pictures concerning the attack. However, this one will make you cringe. A simple tourist getting himself photographed on top of the WTC [World Trade Center] just seconds before the tragedy . . . the camera was found in the rubble!!"[31]

But while at first glance the image seems startling, experts say it is a fake—thus making it a visual urban legend. The photo, experts say, was created with the help of a computer program that enables users to create and alter photographic images.

Real and Not Real

Even though the photo looks genuine, some aspects of it do not ring true, according to David and Barbara Mikkelson, Internet urban legend specialists. For starters, the man is wearing inappropriate clothing for a very warm September morning. Additionally, the researchers note, the observation decks at the World Trade Center did not open before 9:30 a.m., and the first plane hit the building at 8:46 a.m. Further casting doubt on the authenticity of the photo, the airplane shown in the photo is an American Airlines 757, but it was a 767 that hit the North Tower.

Even though the photo is an urban legend, the feelings it provoked were raw and very real, say the Mikkelsons:

> This photo sparked sensations of horror in those who viewed it in the days immediately following the 9/11 attacks on the United States. The image seemingly captured the last fraction of a second of a man's life

. . . and also of the final moment of normalcy before the universe changed for all of us. In the blink of an eye, a beautiful yet ordinary . . . summer day was transformed into flames and falling bodies, buildings collapsing inwards on themselves, and wave upon wave of terror.[32]

What Really Makes an Urban Legend Scary

Experts say that the fear generated in the scariest urban legends does not depend on the amount of blood and gore. It does not necessarily matter whether the person licking the poison envelope glue dies or recovers from the ordeal. The fear comes from the image of ordinary people doing ordinary things—such as driving a car at night, dancing at a wedding, visiting a new place, or sending a letter—and the sudden disaster that befalls them as they engage in these routine acts of daily life.

"It makes us feel for just a moment that the same thing could happen to us," says Marlys Olson:

> If the person were living a kind of risky lifestyle—as a drug addict, a criminal, or even just a guy who hung out with disreputable people—the legend's impact would be less because we'd just tell ourselves, "Well, they were living on the edge, anyway." It's because in the best, scariest urban legends we can see ourselves—or our children or our parents or friends—in that situation, and that randomness of the terror really throws us for a loop. That tingly fear we feel in the pit of our stomachs is *precisely* the big draw of a good scary urban legend.[33]

CHAPTER 3

Celebrity Urban Legends

Hollywood stars, famous musicians, and other celebrities have always generated rumors among the public, so it is not surprising that many of these rumors become widely disseminated urban legends. N.E. Genge calls such urban legends the "big cousins" of celebrity rumors and says: "Scandals, real and imagined, plague people, films, even recording studios. Some are true, some contain a hint of truth, some reflect simple misunderstanding . . . and some are outright lies! Our fascination with celebrities keeps these tales spreading; our love of a good story makes us reluctant to give up the best of these legends, even for the truth."[34]

What Ever Happened To . . . ?

Some of the celebrity legends are about the whereabouts of famous child stars of television shows and movies from the past—especially when those stars retire to a less public life. In many cases the legends have few details, much like the "Did You Know?" urban legends. One widely repeated urban legend concerns the rumored fate of Jerry Mathers, the freckle-faced star of *Leave It to Beaver*, a family sitcom of the 1950s and 1960s—a show that continues in reruns in the twenty-first century.

According to the legend, Mathers, who starred in the show from age 9 to 15, was killed in action in the Vietnam War in 1968. The irony in this story is startling, say Barbara and David Mikkelson. "Urban legends frequently juxtapose concepts such as good and evil, innocence and depravity, safety and danger," they write, "and what could provide a more shocking contrast in opposites than the announcement that one of our best known symbols of innocence and purity had met a violent death in a controversial war?"[35]

Interestingly, this is an example of actual facts giving an urban legend an infusion of energy. Mathers actually did serve in the Air National Guard in the late 1960s, but he never left the United States. When he was invited to be a presenter at the Emmy Awards in 1967, Mathers wore his dress uniform. Therefore, when a soldier with the last name of "Mathers" died in Vietnam in 1968 and some newspapers accidentally reported it as "Jerry Mathers," the story rang true. After all, the American viewing audience had already seen "Beaver" in a military uniform. Even though the mistake was corrected, the legend had already started to spread.

Mr. Rogers—a Marine Sniper?

Another urban legend concerning a television personality involved in war was that involving Fred Rogers, the soft-spoken host of the

award-winning *Mister Rogers' Neighborhood*, a children's show that began in 1967 and still continued in reruns in 2011. In the early 1990s, rumors circulated that Rogers had not always been the soft-spoken man he appeared to be on television. According to the legend, Rogers was actually a skilled sharpshooter who had been a marine sniper in Vietnam, with an impressive 41 confirmed kills to his record—though in some versions the details vary.

"I actually heard it differently,"[36] says Stan Mueller, a former teacher from Milwaukee, Wisconsin, who says he has received two or three e-mails about Rogers's military career. Mueller continues:

> I first heard about it in, I think, 1995 from a coworker, who passed along a letter she'd gotten in the mail from a friend. The letter claimed [Rogers] had been a navy SEAL, not a marine. And I don't remember the number of kills, but the gist of the thing was the same. I guess I never bought into the legend, though—my kids both watched his show, and it didn't seem plausible. One e-mail I got said he was haunted by killing people in that war, so he decided to try to make up for it by helping kids, when the war was over.[37]

Unlike the Mathers legend, however, there are absolutely no facts that might have been misinterpreted by people who first began the urban legend. Rogers, an ordained Presbyterian minister, never served in the military. His career was almost completely devoted to broadcasting and advocating for children. News of Rogers's death in 2003 resulted in recycled versions of the legend—which continue with the reruns of his television series. One e-mail stated in 2003:

> There was this wimpy little man (who just passed away) on PBS, gentle and quiet. Mr. Rogers is another of those you would least suspect of being anything but what he now portrays to our youth. But Mr. Rogers was a U.S. Navy Seal, combat-proven in Vietnam with over twenty-five confirmed kills to his name. He wore a long-sleeve sweater to cover the many tattoos on his forearm and biceps. [He was] a master in small arms and hand-to-hand combat, able to disarm or kill in a heartbeat. He hid that away and won our hearts with his quiet wit and charm.[38]

Oprah Versus Tommy Hilfiger

Some negative celebrity legends have been so widely spread that they have actually damaged the reputations of some famous people. One of the longest lasting of these involves television host Oprah Winfrey and famous fashion designer Tommy Hilfiger. According to the legend, Hilfiger appeared on Winfrey's show in 2000—and delivered a bombshell.

A widely distributed e-mail sent out that year stated that Winfrey had invited Hilfiger on her show to question him about racially offensive comments he supposedly made. The e-mail states: "On the show, she asked him if he had said 'If I had known African-Americans, Hispanics, Jews and Asians would buy my clothes, I would not have made them so nice. I wish these people would not buy my clothes, as they are made for upper-class white

Fashion designer Tommy Hilfiger appeared in a television interview with Oprah Winfrey (pictured) to refute the urban legend that he had made disparaging remarks about African Americans, Hispanics, Jews, and Asians buying his clothing.

people.' His answer to Oprah was a simple 'Yes' when she asked him, and then she immediately asked him to leave her show."[39]

The fallout from that urban legend was swift, sparking a flurry of e-mails and letters written by people who claimed to have seen Winfrey's show when Hilfiger made those comments. Many of these e-mails suggested that people boycott Tommy Hilfiger products as a way of protesting his narrow-minded views. "My suggestion?" said one. "Don't buy your next shirt or perfume from Tommy Hilfiger. Let's give him what he asked for: Let's not buy his clothes, let's put him in a financial state where he himself will NOT be able to afford the ridiculous prices he puts on his clothes. BOYCOTT PLEASE . . ., & SEND THIS MESSAGE TO ANYONE YOU KNOW."[40]

"A Big Fat Lie"

However, not only had Hilfiger never uttered those remarks, he had never appeared on Winfrey's show—at least not until 2006, when she invited him to appear in order to put that urban legend to rest. According to the following transcript of part of that interview, both Winfrey and Hilfiger unequivocally denied the story:

> Oprah: Let's break this down. Tommy, in the 21 years that we've been on the air, have you ever been on the show before today?
> Tommy: Unfortunately, not.
>
> Oprah: And when you first heard it [the comments attributed to him], Tommy, what did you think?
>
> Tommy: I didn't believe it. . . . Friends of mine said they heard the rumor. I said, "That's crazy. That can't be. I was never on the Oprah show. I would never say that." And all my friends and family who know me and people who work with me and people who have grown up with me said that's crazy.
>
> Oprah: Well, did you ever say anything close to that? Where do you think this originated?
>
> Tommy: I have no idea. We hired FBI agents, I did an investigation, I paid investigators lots of money to go out and investigate, and they traced it back to a college campus but couldn't put their finger on it.[41]

Hilfiger was quick to acknowledge that the urban legend had been hurtful. "I wanted to sell a lot of clothes to a lot of people. It hurt my integrity, because at the end of the day, that's all you have. And if people are going to challenge my honesty and my integrity and what I am as a person, it hurts more than anything else," he said. "Forget the money that it has cost me."[42]

At the interview's end, Winfrey had advice for the audience: "The next time somebody sends you an e-mail or somebody mentions this rumor to you, you know what you're supposed say to them?" Winfrey says. "You're supposed to say, 'That's a big fat lie.'"[43]

Embarrassment with an Ice Cream Cone

Not all celebrity urban legends are negative, however. Some involve a chance encounter with a famous movie star. One that has appeared in several variations since the mid-1980s occurs in a Baskin-Robbins ice cream store. The location changes in the variations, but it is always in a part of the United States where one would not necessarily expect to see a famous movie star.

One such story supposedly involves a 33-year-old teacher. According to that story, the woman walks into an ice cream store on a hot, muggy day in Westport, Connecticut. As she is waiting to order, she is stunned to notice that the man who has come in behind her is the famous movie star Paul Newman. The woman later recalls:

> Determined not to get flustered by his presence, I ordered my ice cream, paid for it, and walked outside—only to discover I couldn't find it. When I walked back into the shop, everybody was laughing. Paul grinned at me and said, "It's in your purse." Sure enough, rocky road was melting all

Officially Pronounced Dead

One often-cited clue that Paul McCartney was actually dead before the 1967 release of the *Sgt. Pepper's Lonely Hearts Club Band* album is a patch he is wearing in a photograph inside the album, with the letters *OPD* on it. Fans learned that *OPD* stands for "officially pronounced dead" and is used by British police the way *DOA* (dead on arrival) is used by American police departments.

When asked about the patch after the rumors of his death began circulating, McCartney said, "It is all bloody stupid. I picked up that O.P.D. badge in Canada. It was a police badge. Maybe it means Ontario Police Department or something."

Quoted in John Neary, "The Magical McCartney Mystery," *Life*, November 7, 1969, p. 105.

over the inside of my bag while I turned cherry red
from embarrassment! But Paul couldn't have been
nicer.[44]

Over the years, this legend has featured a variety of celebrities, including Robert Redford, Denzel Washington, Ben Affleck,
Jack Nicholson, and Johnny Depp. When asked about the story,
all have denied that it ever occurred. And, as with most urban
legends, the woman in the story always seems to be "the friend
of a friend," so it is impossible to determine her identity.

The Encounter of a Lifetime

No celebrity encounter was ever as lucky as that featured in
an urban legend known as "The Grateful Millionaire." It seems
that one stormy evening, a school maintenance worker named
Leo Martinez is driving home from work in his pickup after a
long day. As he drives along a stretch of rural highway, he sees a
white stretch limousine on the side of the road. The chauffeur is
struggling to change a flat tire—but without success, for the mud
is not solid enough to support the jack.

Martinez stops and offers to help. He has a sturdy piece of
plywood in the truck, which he places between the mud and the
jack. Within a few minutes, the two men are able to change the
tire. As Martinez heads back to his truck, the chauffeur calls to
him to come back, saying that the man inside the limo wants
to thank him personally. When Martinez reaches the limo and
sticks his head inside, he is stunned to see that the passenger is
billionaire developer and television personality Donald Trump.

Trump thanks Martinez for his kindness and asks if there is
anything he can do for him. Martinez thinks for a moment and
then tells Trump that it is his fifteenth wedding anniversary, and

if Trump would send some flowers to his wife, she would really get a kick out of it. Trump takes down Martinez's address and agrees to send the flowers.

The next afternoon, Martinez's wife meets him at the front door with an amazed smile. Not only has Trump sent a beautiful bouquet, but he has also enclosed a note saying that flowers seemed an inadequate thank-you for such an act of kindness. Therefore, Trump wrote, he has taken the liberty of paying off the mortgage on their home.

A Variety of Grateful Millionaires

As with many other urban legends, "The Grateful Millionaire" has several versions. A 2000 legend that circulated via the Internet had the same basic story, but different details:

> Apparently a couple returning home from a skiing trip in British Columbia spots a disabled car at the side of the road and a man in distress. Being good citizens, they stop to help. . . . The man was grateful, but he had no cash with him to reward them, so asked for their name and address so he could send them a little something. A week later the couple receives a call from their banker saying that their mortgage had been paid and $10,000 had been deposited in their account by a very grateful Bill Gates.[45]

Gates, the founder of Microsoft, and Trump, the wealthy celebrity, are not the only stars of this urban legend. Variations over the years have featured others as the grateful and generous millionaire, including boxer Muhammad Ali, television personality

There is an urban
legend that Jon
Heder of *Napoleon
Dynamite* died in
a drunk driving
accident.

Barbara Walters, musician Nat King Cole, musician Justin Timberlake, and an unnamed Saudi prince visiting the United States. But while the idea of a millionaire rewarding an ordinary citizen for doing him or her a favor is an appealing one, urban legend experts have not been able to verify any of these stories.

Dead Celebrities

Though there are many types of celebrity legends, the most common are the frequent Internet reports of celebrity deaths. In these legends, the celebrity is almost always youthful and apparently healthy but dies suddenly in a surprising manner—often in a way that contradicts his or her public image. One story that began in January 2005, for instance, involved Jon Heder, the star of the movie *Napoleon Dynamite*. Internet postings by a fictitious news agency reported that Heder had been killed in a car crash. According to that posting, the 26-year-old Heder and a companion were driving to Salem, Oregon, when they swerved to avoid hitting a deer and ended up driving off a steep embankment.

It was the circumstances of the crash that most shocked Heder's fans. Some Internet reports stated that ambulance crews had discovered open bottles of liquor in the vehicle, while others alleged that an autopsy revealed the presence of crack cocaine in Heder's system when he died. Both of these reports contrasted with Heder's public acknowledgment of his Mormon faith, which prohibits using drugs of any kind—including alcohol. The legend of Heder's death spread quickly, though it was debunked weeks later—to the relief of his many fans.

One phony death legend that has surfaced repeatedly on the Internet involves Jared Fogle, spokesperson for the Subway food chain since 2000. While in college, Fogle had lost 245 pounds

(111kg) by combining a lot of walking with eating Subway sandwiches for lunch and dinner every day. When his story came to the attention of the Subway corporation, they hired him to do commercials.

By 2007, however, an urban legend began circulating over the Internet that Fogle had died—and that the cause of his death was "abnormal abdominal adhesions resulting from his 1998 gastric bypass surgery."[46] In fact, Fogle is alive and well. He did *not* have gastric bypass surgery, and his claim that he lost all of that weight by exercising and eating a regimen of Subway sandwiches is absolutely true.

Is Paul McCartney Dead?

While many "dead celebrity" urban legends have been told through the years, none has been as widespread nor burned as white-hot as the one that exploded in the headlines in late 1969. In September of that year, just after the release of the new Beatles album *Abbey Road*, fans began hearing rumors that the band's bass guitarist, Paul McCartney, was dead. According to the story, he had died in an automobile crash almost three years before the album's release. However, because the band was so incredibly successful, the other three Beatles, John Lennon, George Harrison, and Ringo Starr, decided to keep the death a secret. They agreed to continue their recording dates and other appearances using a musician that looked and sounded enough like McCartney to be plausible.

For the most part, this story seemed incredible, yet certain facts left Beatles fans wondering. For example, there had been rumors that the Beatles were about to break up because they could not agree on the band's future direction. Perhaps, thought some fans, the group was considering disbanding not because of a disagreement but because it was becoming more and more difficult to keep McCartney's death secret. Even more telling, though they continued to record their music, the Beatles had stopped touring by 1967, which made them far less visible to the public. McCartney, who was said to be living on a farm in a remote part of Scotland with his wife and children, was especially absent from public view. These and other bits of the story added some measure of believability to the idea that McCartney had died years before.

Searching for Clues

The death of McCartney might have been just a passing urban legend like so many others if not for more rumors that there were actually clues pointing to his death contained in some of the albums the band had released since 1966. In the weeks that followed the initial rumor of McCartney's death, wrote *Life* reporter John Neary, thousands and thousands of fans spent long periods of time "studying Beatle record album jackets with the meticulous scrutiny of CIA photo-interpreters microscoping aerials of enemy missile sites. They had spiraled down the grooves of every Beatle record ever cut speeding them up from 33 to 45 rpm, to 78, slowing them to 16—even taping them and reversing the tapes, analyzing stereo recordings track by track."[47]

Though it sounds outlandish, such work produced some results that were hard to ignore. At the end of the song "Strawberry Fields Forever," for example, many listeners believed they could hear Lennon's voice saying, "I buried Paul." Another eerie clue, some believed, was in "Revolution 9," a song on *The White Album*. During the song, there is a nine-minute hodgepodge of sounds, during which a man's voice repeatedly intones,

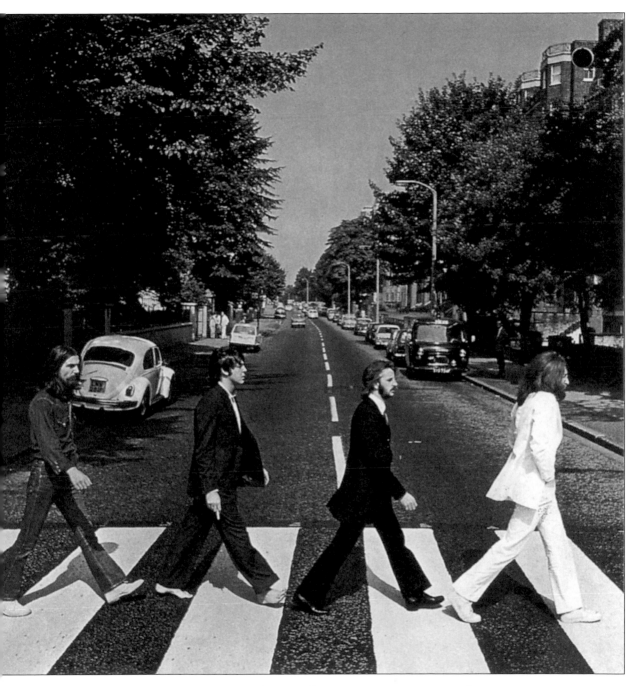

For years, an urban legend claimed that Beatles singer-songwriter Paul McCartney was dead. Although McCartney is still very much alive, details on the cover of the group's Abbey Road record album seemed to support the story that all was not right with McCartney.

"Number nine, number nine, number nine." If that section is played in reverse, notes Neary, "a quite different voice will be heard to say, "Turn me on, dead man, turn me on, dead man.""[48]

Louis Yager, president of the Is Paul McCartney Dead Society at Hofstra University, maintained in 1969 that there was no other explanation for the clues. "I mean, it's all right there,"[49] he said.

Photo Evidence?

Many believed that some of the most compelling evidence was in the photographs contained in the albums. "Paul—or maybe it was his double—was different than the others in a bunch of the photos," says child-care worker Vicky Hennigan, who was a senior in high school when the rumor started. "In one, [McCartney] had his back to the camera while the other three were facing forward. Or he had a black flower when the others had red ones. It seemed believable to me."[50]

Hennigan says she was most interested in the cover of *Abbey Road*, which showed the four Beatles walking across a busy London street. She says:

> Each of them was dressed in what seemed like real symbolic clothing. There was Paul in a scruffy suit, barefoot, as a corpse might be; George, in workman's clothes, like a gravedigger, Ringo in a dark suit—I guess he was the mourner at the funeral, and John all in white—like a minister. Plus, if you looked carefully, you could see Paul was the only one of the four who was out of step in the photo. Too much stuff there to be coincidental, you know?[51]

Many fans wondered why, if Mc-Cartney had not been killed, there were so many apparent clues within the albums. Ron Heinz, a Minnesota human resources worker, remembers thinking that the Beatles were so intelligent and so creative that they might have even had a part in starting the whole story. "The Beatles were pre-eminent celebrities of their time," he says, "and given their mystical, transcendental experiences, I thought it might not be beyond the Beatles to communicate a cover-up to their fans in this puzzling way."[52]

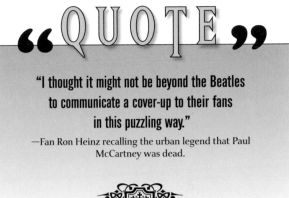

Not Dead

The Paul-is-dead stories started to decline, however, when *Life* magazine published a new interview with McCartney in November 1969. In the interview, he told London *Life* correspondent Dorothy Bacon: "Perhaps the rumour started because I haven't been much in the press lately. I have done enough press for a lifetime, and I don't have anything to say these days. I am happy to be with my family and I will work when I work. I was switched on for ten years and I never switched off. Now I am switching off whenever I can. I would rather be a little less famous these days"[53]

As far as why there were so many aural and visual hints that seemed to support the urban legend, the Beatles and their agents could offer no explanation and maintained that there was nothing at all to it. Trying to put the legend to rest, Beatles drummer Starr remarked, "It's a load of old crap."[54]

CHAPTER 4

Animal Urban Legends

Because most people love hearing about animals (especially pets), it is no surprise that they play a large part in many urban legends. According to urban legend experts Gillian Bennett and Paul Smith, about 20 percent of urban legends are about animals. From creepy-crawlies like spiders, roaches, and centipedes to birds, reptiles, and family pets like cats and dogs, animals occupy a place in some of the most enduring legends.

Alligators in the Sewers

No urban legend involving animals has been as long lasting in the United States as the legend that hundreds—perhaps thousands—of alligators live beneath the streets of New York City. In fact, many modern folklorists say that this particular story has become synonymous with the term *urban legend*.

As the story goes, thousand of alligators thrive in New York City sewers. Their presence dates back to the 1920s, when tourists traveling to Florida began bringing back baby alligators as souvenirs for their children. As the little alligators continued to grow—and bite—some families gave them to zoos; others flushed them down the toilet.

The result, the story goes, is that the alligators found themselves in a new environment that was not entirely unfriendly. Although for certain months of the year it was far colder than the tropical climate alligators are used to, there was a plentiful supply of food. Not only could the growing alligators feed off smaller alligators, they could eat sewer rats as well as garbage that made its way into the sewers. Over the years, the alligators gradually grew blind from being in the constant darkness, and because their skin was never exposed to sunlight, they (and their offspring) lost their pigment, leaving them a whitish-gray color. Some, the legend says, are so big they could easily kill and eat a sewer worker unlucky enough to encounter one.

Dubious Beginnings

The earliest published reference to the presence of alligators in New York's sewers was a book by Robert Daley titled *World Beneath the City.* Daley interviewed Teddy May, a previous superintendent of sewers in New York. May agreed that the story sounded bogus, but insisted that he had seen the sewer-dwelling alligators with his own eyes.

Years later, however, when folklorist Jan Harold Brunvand was investigating the urban legend, he met a New York sewer official named John T. Flaherty, who scoffed at the idea of

"It's a myth that will never die."

—Cathy DelliCarpini of the New York Department of Environmental Protection, on the urban legend that alligators have infested that city's sewers.

alligators in the sewers. Without being overly critical, Flaherty verified that May indeed worked for the Bureau of Sewers, but as for his trustworthiness, said, "Teddy was a very outgoing, ebullient man with a wide circle of friends. . . . Part of his charm was his undoubted abilities as a raconteur and a spinner of yarns."[55]

Still, the idea that the sewers are teeming with giant white alligators is one that continues, no matter how many times experts say that it is not true. Animal experts have explained that not only was it far too cold for alligators, the presence of dangerous bacteria such as E. coli and salmonella in the sewers would kill them off very quickly. Even with such explanations, the Bureau of Sewers gets calls from people every year wondering about the alligators. Says Cathy DelliCarpini, a spokesperson for New York's Department of Environmental Protection, which has spent more than 30 years debunking the legend, "It's a myth that will never die."[56]

The Brave Deerhound

The interaction between people and their pets—most often dogs—is a popular subject of urban legends. Many animal legends involve a misunderstanding or mistake in judgment on the part of humans—an error that later proves to have tragic consequences.

Some folklorists point to one particular legend that likely has spawned dozens of today's urban legends—though it happened many centuries ago. A most poignant telling of this legend is from thirteenth-century Wales, though there have been similar stories in the folklore of Greece, India, Israel, and Russia.

The story is about Gelert, a beautiful, fawn-colored deerhound. His owner, a prince named Llewellyn, is convinced that there has never been a dog as smart and brave as Gelert. The dog

OPPOSITE:
Thousands of alligators thrive in New York City sewers, according to one enduring urban legend. They are, the story goes, the unfortunate result of people bringing home baby alligators (pictured) as exotic vacation souvenirs and then flushing them down toilets once the creatures start to grow.

is courageous and tireless when they are hunting, but at home he is as meek as a lamb—especially with Llewellyn's year-old son. No matter how roughly the boy plays, no matter if he pulls the dog's tail or jumps on him, Gelert is always gentle.

One day, Prince Llewellyn blows his trumpet to call Gelert, but the dog does not come—something that has never happened before. He blows the trumpet again and again, but no answering bark comes from the dog. Llewellyn, angry that the dog is being disobedient, goes hunting without Gelert. When he returns home, Gelert walks through the door, a bit unsteadily, to meet his master. Llewellyn is horrified to see the dog's mouth covered in blood. As he walks into the palace, he notices a trail of blood leading to his son's nursery. Once in the nursery he sees the floor covered in blood and no sign of his little boy.

Convinced that the dog has killed his son, Llewellyn draws his sword and screams at Gelert, calling him a monster, and then plunges his sword into the dog's side. Gelert lies dying, his sad eyes on his master's face. As the dog struggles to take his last breath, Llewellyn is shocked to hear the cries of his son. He runs toward the sound into an adjoining room and is speechless at what he sees: Not only is his son alive and unharmed, but beside him are the bloody remains of a wolf. His faithful dog Gelert risked his life to save the little boy and, instead of being rewarded, was savagely killed by his own master. Grieving and ashamed, Llewellyn buries the dog outside the palace walls; the place today is known as Beddgelert, Welsh for "the grave of Gelert."

Not Nearly as Serious

The idea of a beloved dog accidentally suffering at the hand of its owner has changed since thirteenth-century Wales, not only in the details of the story but in the tone. While the moral or message may still warn humans to think before they act rashly with their animal companions, the desired effect is much different. The following legend about two friends, Ed and Bill, who decide to go duck hunting was spread by e-mail beginning in 2002 and continued into 2010. Though the ending is tragic and the moral the same as that of the story of Gelert, this urban legend seems intended to be darkly humorous.

Neither of the two men has ever actually been duck hunting, but they are confident that they can catch on pretty quickly. Ed drives, since he has a big new Lincoln Navigator, a very expensive luxury SUV that can easily accommodate the hunters, their hunting equipment, and Ed's Labrador retriever. Because it is late in the duck-hunting season, they are able to drive right onto the thick ice of the lake. The men decide to use a stick of dynamite to blast a hole in the lake, where they can set up their duck decoys.

Ed lights the dynamite, which has a 40-second fuse, and tosses it as far as he can. His Lab—an excellent retriever—then does what many Labs do well: He speeds toward the falling stick and catches it just as it reaches the ice. He then lopes toward his master with the dynamite in his mouth as the terrified hunters watch. Ed shoots his gun over the dog's head, hoping to frighten him away. Frightened and confused, the dog takes cover under the only large object he sees—the Navigator.

"At the kaboom," writes Byron Stout of Florida's *News Press*, who first read this fictional story on the Internet, "the dog and the $42,500 SUV were destroyed as the ice crumbled and the whole works plummeted to the bottom of the lake. If the loss of a faithful dog was not enough, the owner of the Navigator was

A lot of urban legends imply that certain cultures are not trustworthy.

informed by his insurance policy that sinking a vehicle by the illegal use of explosives was not covered by his policy."[57]

"The Mexican Pet"

One of the most famous modern animal legends is about the riskiness of finding a suitable pet and the unforeseen dangers that can befall American travelers. It begins as a middle-aged American woman named Laura takes a weeklong vacation in Mexico.

Each time she goes in or out of her hotel room, Laura notices a scrawny, obviously malnourished dog outside her door. She has heard that in Mexico dogs are considered more of a nuisance than beloved pets; she has seen street vendors throwing rocks at dogs who come too close to their carts. But this particular dog looks so vulnerable, she knows she has to do something. She decides to save leftovers from her meals to give the little dog when she returns to the room.

Though the dog seems nervous about approaching her at first, he soon begins to bond with Laura. He comes into the room and sits obediently at the side of the bed while she reads or watches television. He does not seem to belong to any guest or hotel worker. So at the end of the week, Laura decides to do something daring—she smuggles the little dog across the border in her straw purse.

A day or two after she returns home, Laura wakes to find the dog—whom she has named Amigo—in obvious distress. His eyes are oozing and matted, and he seems to be having trouble breathing. Frantic, she calls a nearby veterinarian, who tells Laura to bring Amigo in right away.

When she arrives, she fears the worst. His breathing is raspy

In one urban legend which has several variations, a scrawny, malnourished animal encountered on a Mexican vacation is smuggled into the United States by a woman who believes she has found the perfect pet. She is later horrified to learn that her sweet little dog is actually a sewer rat.

and he seems restless. Tearfully, she asks the vet if he can save her little dog. When he asks where she got the animal, she at first says that she picked him out in a shelter. He then tells her there is no way she acquired Amigo in the United States, and he asks her again where she got the animal.

Embarrassed, she admits the dog is a stray that she illegally brought home from Mexico. Laura expects a lecture on the foolishness of doing something illegal. What she gets instead is the news that the creature she smuggled across the border in her purse is not a dog but a very large Mexican sewer rat. And it is dying—of rabies.

Variations on a Theme

Experts say that there are more than a dozen variations of "The Mexican Pet." In one the woman is confused when she cannot find her cat (who is twice the size of her new pet.) Suspicious when Amigo seems to have gained weight rather quickly, the woman is revolted when she discovers bones and tufts of the cat's fur in the cushions of Amigo's bedding.

In another variation the woman learns that the pet is a sewer rat rather than a dog after she discovers the animal chewing the ear of her two-year-old son. In several of the variations, a veterinarian euthanizes the new pet after explaining that sewer rats are extremely vicious and are able to kill and consume animals twice their size—although they are extremely calm around humans.

Folklorists point out that while the details of the story differ, the implied moral does not, as Marlys Olson notes:

> It's another version of the "Don't trust those foreign countries" theme. You see versions of ["The Mexican Pet"] in which the innocent woman is Ukrainian, and is traveling in India, or Egypt, or sometimes it's a Canadian woman in Thailand. The message is that really ugly, disgusting things can happen to an unwary traveler in these untrustworthy places. It's a pretty common theme running through these types of urban legends—that some cultures are by nature very suspect, and the less we interact with them, the safer we are.[58]

"Bunny Bounces Back"

A less gruesome, but more ironic animal urban legend began circulating in the 1980s in Scotland, Wales, and New Zealand.

New versions have appeared via e-mail in the twenty-first century. The story involves a woman who goes to the back door to let her dog in and discovers a large, dead rabbit in the hound's mouth.

At first, she thinks little of it, since the vacant lots nearby have been overrun with rabbits and chipmunks for years. But a closer look shows this is no ordinary rabbit. Though muddy and bedraggled, the rabbit is clearly a white Angora—a special breed raised for its long, fluffy wool. It also has a ribbon around its neck. As she stares at it, she recalls that a neighbor girl has just such a rabbit. Realizing the terrible problem, she wonders what she could possibly do.

Going to the neighbors to confess what her dog has done is out of the question—it is simply too embarrassing. Besides, she would have a hard time looking that little girl in the eye, knowing how much she loves that rabbit. So she makes a plan: She carefully washes the dead rabbit and uses the blow dryer to make its coat fluffy and shiny. She replaces the pink ribbon around its neck—now muddy and torn—with a new one from her sewing basket. Satisfied with her work, she conceals the rabbit under her coat and creeps around the back of her neighbor's house. According to an account in Scotland's *Sunday Post*, she "opened the empty rabbit hutch, popped poor bunny in a corner and cosied him up with straw. Then . . . she made good her escape."[59]

A short time later, while enjoying a cup of tea, she hears a scream coming from the neighbor's yard. She rushes out and finds her neighbor frightened and confused. "Look at this," the neighbor screeches. "Our rabbit died two days ago. We buried him in the garden, but now he's sitting up at the back of his hutch!"[60]

A Genre of Mistaken Deaths

There is another story known as "The Poisoned Dinner Party," whose irony is similar to "Bunny Bounces Back." In fact, some

folklorists suspect that the story of a dinner party in Depression-era New York City actually morphed into a series of more modern legends—including "Bunny Bounces Back." Though different in many ways, the idea of an animal's mistaken death is the crux of this old urban legend.

The main character is an uptown Manhattan socialite who decides to throw a beautiful dinner party for nine of her friends. She spares no expense on the food, including fresh salmon, mushroom hors d'oeuvres, and dozens of side dishes and desserts. Moments before the ladies are due to arrive, she notices that her cocker spaniel has somehow jumped onto a table and eaten some of the cuts of salmon. Furious, she hands the dog to the butler, who takes him into a back room.

The hostess forgets all about the mishap as her guests begin to arrive. As they enjoy their meal, the butler walks into the room and whispers to the hostess that the dog has died. Thinking that the dog died because of the salmon, she stands up and announces that the salmon is poisoned and, humiliated, tells everyone what happened before they arrived. According to one version of the legend: "There followed a mad rush to the hospital, with ten beautiful but panic-stricken ladies screaming for stomach pumps at the same time. When the ordeal was over, and it became apparent that they were going to survive, they headed weakly for their homes and sleeping pills."[61]

When the hostess comes home, she tells the butler that she wants to see the body of her beloved dog. Startled, the butler exclaims that she surely would not want to see the dog. After all, the butler tells her, the poor thing had been hit by a truck.

"The Poisoned Dinner Party," like so many other urban legends, spread quickly. In one newspaper article from 1933, a

The Tourist and the Kangaroo

One animal urban legend that has been around for decades and surfaces periodically in e-mails involves a young American tourist who is driving along a highway in the Australian outback hoping to photograph a kangaroo. Ironically, a large gray kangaroo hops onto the road just ahead of the speeding car, but the tourist is unable to stop in time and hits the animal.

Deciding that he can still fulfill his wish to take a photo, the man takes off his sport coat and sunglasses, dresses the kangaroo, and props him up by the car and begins taking photos. As he is busy adjusting the settings on his camera for a final shot, the kangaroo—merely stunned, as it turns out—bounds away. Suddenly, the horrified tourist realizes the kangaroo has just made off with his money, credit cards, and passport—all of which were in his coat pockets. No evidence of this event has ever surfaced; however, many who tell the story contend they know the tourist.

reporter noted that the legend was very well traveled. "People are always popping up," he wrote, "to declare that a friend of their next-door neighbor knows a woman who actually attended that unhappy dinner party."[62]

Photoshop and Animal Urban Legends

Any discussion of animal urban legends would not be complete without looking at the role photography plays in spreading legends on the Internet. Computer programs such as Photoshop enable people to create or manipulate images to suit their needs. For instance, in 2007 an e-mail began circulating on the Internet announcing the world's biggest dog—an English mastiff named Hercules that weighs in at an astonishing 282 pounds (128kg). The e-mail includes a photograph showing a man and a woman walking a horse and the dog through a park. Hercules's head appears as high as the man's chest. The e-mail quotes his owner, named Mr. Flynn, who claims Hercules's weight is natural and not the result of some strange diet. "I fed him normal food," Flynn says, "and he just grew."[63]

But urban legend experts, among others, caution against believing everything that appears on the web. "Thanks to some clever Photoshop manipulation, writes David Emery, "the dog pictured . . . (which actually appears to be a Neapolitan mastiff, not an English mastiff as claimed) looks roughly twice its natural size. It's an obvious hoax."[64]

A Whale of an Adventure?

The majority of doctored animal images seen on the web that have become urban legends show a human in a perilous situation with very dangerous animals, such as one that began showing up in Internet users' in-boxes in 2001. That photo shows a military helicopter poised over the water as a great white shark leaps up to attack it. As the text accompanying the photo explains, "Although this looks like a picture taken from a Hollywood movie, it is in fact a real photo, taken near the South African coast during a military exercise by the British Navy. It has been nominated by [*National Geographic*] as 'THE photo of the year.'"[65]

The photo, however, is a hoax. As *National Geographic News* explained in 2005, the photo was actually created by someone who spliced two photographs together—one of a US Air Force helicopter hovering above San Francisco Bay, and a second photo of a shark taken in South Africa: "The photo of a breaching great white shark was taken by South African photographer Charles Maxwell. . . . The Air Force photo of an HH-60G Pave Hawk helicopter was taken by Lance Cheung. They were spliced together by an unknown person, and reportedly began making the rounds on e-mail in August 2001."[66]

It was a manipulated photo, and though the *National Geographic* website received hundreds of visits daily about the photo, the National Geographic Society made it clear it had never considered it in contention for "Photo of the Year."

An Accidental Urban Legend

Though many manipulated photos are circulated purposely to fool people into believing something extraordinary, occasionally a photo urban legend begins quite unintentionally. That was the case with a photo that circulated in 2010, showing a man kayaking through the gaping mouth of a surfacing humpback whale. In the text accompanying the photo, Robert Kraft of Sitka, Alaska, writes: "Yep, that is me in the picture. Yep, that is a whale that was just around the corner from the ferry terminal. 'Paddle really fast' is the only thing I could think of at the time. Also think-

ing that I don't look like a herring, don't smell like a herring but with the same herring instinct of 'get the hell out of the way of that big mouth!' Still living to tell yet another story."[67]

In fact, the man in the photo *was* Kraft. His friend, photographer Tim Shobe, later explained that the Internet photo was actually two photos—both taken by him. One was of Kraft in his kayak, and the other—the surfacing humpback—was taken three months later, in a different location. "I came up with the idea to create a manipulated image with the help of Photoshop to use as a small piece of entertainment for a few of my friends on my e-mail list,"[68] Shobe explains. Kraft himself forwarded the photo to a few people, too.

Before long, the photo and Shobe's accompanying text took on a life of its own, thanks to the Internet. People everywhere wanted to know how Kraft could have survived the encounter, and they marveled at the quick thinking of the photographer to get such a dramatic shot. According to an article in the *Daily Sitka Sentinel*, "Shobe said he was surprised not only that people took the photo at face value, but also at the wide distribution of his Photoshopped image."[69]

It seems that no matter how far-fetched the tale, there are always people willing to believe—especially when the legend is accompanied by photographic evidence. And as with all the best urban legends, people are always eager to pass the legend along.

CHAPTER 5

Buyer Be Wary!

O f all the varieties and themes of urban legends, people seem to be bothered the most by those dealing with food and beverages. Whether the stories are about suspicious ingredients in certain foods or the reliability of the restaurants or stores that sell them, folklore enthusiast Marlys Olson says they have a profound effect:

> It isn't surprising, really, because food is common to 100 percent of us. An urban legend about Cadillacs or Jaguars might be interesting, but not everyone drives a Cadillac or a Jaguar, so we don't have a personal stake in the outcome of [the urban legend's] message. But food? Absolutely! We all eat. We may not all throw down a hundred dollars for

a meal at an expensive restaurant, but we all have done the drive-through at McDonald's, we all shop for groceries. So these legends speak to all of us— and sometimes a lot louder than we'd wish.[70]

The Yuck Factor

Many of the most unappetizing food legends involve nationally known fast-food restaurants. Since the 1980s people have been spreading urban legends about food contaminated with things that should definitely not be there. These legends capitalize on what many call the "yuck factor"—so named because of the horror and revulsion people have when they hear such stories.

Louise Manning, a retired church secretary in Saskatchewan, Canada, says that she avoided a well-known hamburger chain for years because she had heard that the company used night crawlers and other types of worms to make their hamburgers. "It was a rumor going around years ago that their hamburgers were loaded with worms," she says. Manning continues:

> The story was something about how it didn't make the burgers taste different, but it was cheaper for the company than using 100 percent beef. . . . I think the ration was 70 percent beef, 30 percent worms. A fellow I worked with told me he'd heard they'd done market research studies and found that people couldn't tell the difference. Goodness—I heard that, and I vowed I'd never go in one of those restaurants ever again. It is interesting to me today that long after it was made clear that it wasn't true at all, that it was all an urban myth, I

Several businesses have fallen victim to the urban legend phenomenon. One story making the rounds for a time claimed that a well-known hamburger chain used night crawlers and other worms in their hamburger meat.

still had trouble going [into the restaurant]. Today I will, but I only get the chicken. Isn't that funny? I just can't get that idea of worms out of my head, I guess.[71]

An Easy Target

Every few years a new urban legend surfaces about off-putting ingredients in fast-food hamburgers. Because McDonald's is such a well-known purveyor of fast food throughout the world, it is not surprising that their name is used in so many of the legends.

In 1999, for instance, many people were notified in e-mails that McDonald's was the world's largest purchaser of cow eyeballs—which found their way into hamburgers. The corporation denied that rumor, as they deny all urban legends targeting the purity of their food. The label on all of their beef products states: "Contains 100% pure USDA inspected beef; no additives, no fillers, no extenders."[72]

While millions of people buy meals at fast-food restaurants every week, urban legend researcher David Emery believes many people have an underlying unease about these establishments. He says:

> Let's face it, while most of us do eat fast food of one sort or another for the sake of convenience, we don't really trust it. We don't trust it because it's cheap, it's mass-produced, and it's sold to us by vast, impersonal corporations that don't necessarily have our best interests at heart. . . . Sharing fast food horror stories—of which "Icky Hamburger Additives" makes up a major subgenre—is one way we express our collective misgivings about our eating habits in the 21st Century.[73]

Frankenchickens

Urban legends about disgusting ingredients in food circulate about many other fast-food restaurants, too. In 1991 the Kentucky

Fried Chicken company shortened its brand name to KFC, and it was not long before a new urban legend was born. Some observers speculated at the time that the change was done to downplay the "fried" aspect of the food, in an effort to make it seem healthier. However, according to several e-mails that began circulating in the late 1990s—and were appearing as recently as 2010—the reason was actually something very sinister.

According to the story, KFC had stopped using chickens entirely —at least, real chickens. Instead, they were using genetically engineered organisms that their research scientists had developed—something that tasted like chicken but did not require butchering, since it was mostly meat. As the e-mail explains:

> These so called "chickens" are kept alive by tubes inserted into their bodies to pump blood and nutrients throughout their structure. They have no beaks, no feathers, and no feet. Their bone structure is dramatically shrunk to get more meat out of them. This is great for KFC because they do not have to pay so much for their production costs. There is no more plucking of the feathers or the removal of the beaks and feet.

> The government has told them to change all of their menus so they do not say chicken anywhere. If you look closely you will notice this. Listen to their commercials, I guarantee you will not see or hear the word chicken. I find this matter to be very disturbing. I hope people will start to realize this and let other people know.[74]

Did You Know?

Pop Rocks and soda pop cannot make one's stomach explode.

Executives at KFC headquarters continue to be astonished at the idea that some people might be taking the urban legend seriously. When Emery asked Michael Tierney, KFC's director of public affairs, if there was even a shred of truth to the story, Tierney was succinct. "Of course not," he said. "Any thinking adult would know it's absolutely absurd."[75]

Disgusting Extras

Sometimes an urban legend focuses not on the ingredients used to make a certain food, but rather on the accidental addition of something disgusting in the processing, serving, or packaging of that product. These stories, casting doubt on the purity and safety of food, add a shiver of fear to the way people think about something they usually take for granted.

For instance, some legends tell about a man who finds the remains of a dead mouse in his bottle of Coca-Cola, or a woman who reaches into a bucket of Kentucky Fried Chicken and, to her horror, pulls out an "extra-crispy" chicken head, complete with comb and beak. Another legend tells of a man who finds several bloody bandages on the pizza he ordered from a well-known chain. Most of these stories turn out to be urban legends—popular to repeat and spread because they are almost guaranteed to both fascinate and repel listeners.

Shreds of Truth?

However, one of the reasons so many food legends are so horrific to hear is that there have actually been cases where people *have* found foul things in their food or drinks. In 2009, for example, a Florida man was shocked after he noticed an odd taste in the can of Diet Pepsi he was drinking. It turned out there were the remains of a dead animal in the can—first believed to be a mouse, but later identified as a frog or toad.

Restaurants and food producers are leery of such stories. If contamination occurs, they say, it almost always happens after the consumer opens the can or package. In some cases, people have purposely contaminated their own food in an effort to win a large cash settlement from a restaurant chain or corporation.

That very thing happened in 2005 at a Wendy's restaurant in San Jose, California, when a woman found what appeared to be part of a human finger in the cup of chili she was eating. Though Anna Ayala at first insisted that she was only an innocent victim, she finally admitted that she put the finger in her own food. Her husband, Jaime Placencia, had obtained the severed finger from a coworker, who lost it in an industrial accident. Believing they could sue Wendy's and be compensated, Ayala pretended the finger was already in the chili when she purchased it.

Ayala and Placencia were given prison sentences for their actions. And, as so often happens in such cases, though Wendy's was not at all responsible for the finger being in the chili, the company's reputation suffered as a result. The price of the urban rumors that circulated before the facts were known was an estimated $21 million in lost business.

Pop Rocks and Soda

Wendy's had no trouble regaining its footing after the chili incident; however, a candy called Pop Rocks had a much harder time. First introduced by General Foods in 1975, Pop Rocks are tiny pieces of candy made with little pockets of carbon dioxide (the same gas used in soda pop) that is released when the candy melts in one's mouth—creating a popping sound. At 15¢ a pack,

"Any thinking adult would know it's absolutely absurd."

—KFC spokesperson Michael Tierney, responding to the "Frankenchicken" rumor.

No Eyeballs in Hamburgers

On the website About.com, urban legend researcher David Emery examines a popular urban legend and offers a factual economic argument for why it could not be true.

> Contrary to popular assumption, bovine eyeballs can fetch a higher price on the open market than the choicest cuts of beef. That's because they're in demand at research facilities and college biology labs for experimental purposes. At one

and with flavors like grape, orange, and cherry, they were an immediate hit with kids of all ages.

But even though Pop Rocks had been tested and found completely harmless, some consumers were nervous about them. The Food and Drug Administration set up a hotline for people to online biological supply house I checked (yes, you can buy cow eyeballs over the Internet!), the going rate, in bulk, was over $2 apiece. Similarly, earthworms—another alleged low-cost substitute for beef in fast food burgers—are way more expensive than beef itself.

If, in fact, McDonald's were the world's largest purchaser of cow eyeballs, we could only surmise that the burger chain is engaged in some sort of very expensive, super-secret scientific research—a horror story unto itself.

David Emery, "Is McDonald's the World's Biggest Purchaser of Cow Eyeballs?," About.com, 2011. http://urbanlegends.about.com.

call and ask questions about the candy. Even so, some people remained suspicious about the safety of the candy, and by the late 1970s unsettling urban legends began to spread.

One persistent story claims that by mixing Pop Rocks and soda, one can create an unhealthy amount of carbonation. A person who drinks this concoction would produce powerful, painful belches—at the very least. Even more disturbing, according to one legend, consuming too much of the mixture of soda and Pop Rocks could be fatal. Explains the website Timeless Myths, "The gas build up comes on too fast, causing the stomach to explode, resulting in a horrible death."[76]

The Death of Mikey

The urban legend about the dangers of Pop Rocks got a boost in 1979 when—according to a new legend—a well-known child actually died from combining the candy and soda. The chubby-cheeked, freckle-faced boy was known to television viewers as Mikey. He was an actor who appeared in a commercial for Life cereal beginning in 1971.

The boy who played Mikey at the age of three never achieved much fame outside of that commercial, and by the late 1970s had seemingly vanished from sight. This gave the rumor of his Pop Rocks death credibility, and sales of the candy began to suffer. Despite an effort to dispel the myth about the dangers of their product by taking out full-page ads in dozens of newspapers across the country and mailing explanatory letters to 50,000 school principals, misinformation prevailed, and General Foods decided to pull Pop Rocks from the market in 1983.

Though the candy disappeared for awhile, it was reintroduced five years later under a the new name Action Candy, and as currently as 2011, is marketed under its original name of Pop Rocks. Despite all these measures, the urban legend of the dangers of Pop Rock and soda, as well as the death of Mikey, still circulate, though not as widely.

An urban legend that began circulating by e-mail in the late 1990s—and was still around as of 2010—claimed that the fried chicken establishment KFC was using genetically engineered organisms rather than real chickens. The company refutes the story, saying it is utterly absurd.

"The Biscuit Bullet"

Some of the most interesting urban legends involving food products are not necessarily about what happens when one eats the food, but about the dangers of the packaging. One such legend, widely known as "The Biscuit Bullet," begins when Mike, a New Jersey 16-year-old, sees a woman sitting in her car in a shopping center parking lot. Though it is a very hot day, he notices that the woman is sitting in the driver's seat with the windows shut and her eyes closed. She has her hands clasped behind her head, which seems odd to him.

When Mike comes out of the grocery store a few minutes later, she is still there, with her hands still clasped behind her head. He taps on the window, but she does not respond. Unsure what he should do—but worried that she might be ill, or even dead—he uses his cell phone to call 911. A squad car is the first to arrive, and the woman rolls down her window.

In a weak, quavering voice, she tells the officer that she has been sitting there almost an hour. She says that when she first returned to her car after shopping, she heard a loud bang and felt a sudden pain in the back of her head. In one version of the story, the woman tells the police, "I've been shot in the head, and I am holding my brains in."[77]

Puzzled at the lack of blood, as well as doubtful the woman would be conscious with such trauma to her brain, the officer takes a look. What he sees is a gooey, tannish mass—but it is not her brain. He also sees the remnants of a tube covered in shiny, blue paper—a tube that once held Pillsbury biscuit dough. He assures her that she is not losing her brains; the loud bang was the tube exploding (probably in the hot car) as the dough hit her in the back of the head.

A $250 Recipe

At least one urban food legend started not because of food that was bad or contaminated, but rather because of food that was delicious. According to the legend, which began circulating by e-mail in 1996, a customer at the restaurant of a Neiman Marcus department store in Dallas, Texas, asks for a recipe for one of the items on the menu—with astonishing results.

After doing some shopping, the woman and her daughter go into the store's restaurant for lunch. After a salad, they decide to try something called the Neiman Marcus Cookie and are both wowed by how wonderful it tastes. When the woman asks their server for the recipe, she is told that the store's policy is to sell the recipe, not give it away. When asked how much it would cost, the server tells her, "Two-fifty."[78] Deciding it is a steal for $2.50, the woman asks the server to put it on her meal tab and leaves with the recipe in her purse.

At the end of the month she notices an odd charge on her monthly credit card statement from Neiman Marcus. She writes in an e-mail:

> As I glanced at the bottom of the statement, it said, "Cookie Recipe-$250.00." That's outrageous!! I called Neiman's Accounting Dept. and told them the waitress said it was "two-fifty," which clearly does not mean "two hundred and fifty dollars" by any possible interpretation of the phrase. Neiman Marcus refused to budge. . . . They would not refund my money, because according to them, "What the waitress told you is not our problem. You have already seen

A woman was
sentenced to nine
years in prison in
2005 for putting a
human finger in her
Wendy's chili, and
pretending
that it was in the
chili when she
purchased it.

the recipe—we absolutely will not refund your money at this point."[79]

"$250 Worth of Fun"

The woman is furious and reminds the accounting department worker that there are specific statutes that prohibit fraud in the state of Texas, and she threatens to report the store to the Better Business Bureau. However, the store employee is not concerned. "I was basically told, 'Do what you want, we don't give a damn, and we're not refunding your money,'" she writes. "I waited a moment, thinking of how I could get even, or even try to get any of my money back. I just said, 'Okay, you folks got my $250, and now I'm going to have $250 worth of fun."

She tells the woman that she is going to e-mail the recipe to everyone she knows and make sure those friends send it on to their friends, too. "I told her that I was going to see to it that every cookie lover in the United States with an e-mail account has a $250.00 cookie recipe from Neiman-Marcus . . . for free."[80]

Though the Neiman Marcus account worker protests that she should not do that, the woman is unmoved. "Well," she says, "you should have thought of that before you ripped me off." The story ends as the woman includes the recipe in her e-mail, writing, "So here it is!!! Please, please, please pass it on to everyone you can possibly think of. I paid $250.00 for this . . . I don't want Neiman Marcus to ever get another penny off this recipe."[81]

Folklorists say this is a long-running urban legend. In the 1990s and early twenty-first century, the villain was Neiman Marcus, but in the 1980s it was the Mrs. Fields cookie chain. Actually, the oldest version of this urban legend has its roots not in cookies, but rather a particularly tasty red velvet cake from New York City's Waldorf Astoria Hotel in 1948. The current version, notes David Emery, "is still making the online rounds, and its popularity shows no sign of waning despite repeated debunkings over the past two decades."[82]

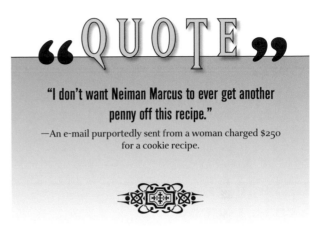

Truth Fighting a Losing Battle

As with all widely spread urban legends, food-based rumors are difficult to combat. It seems ironic, since there are scores of books about urban legends and several respected, thorough websites on the Internet dedicated to dispelling hundreds of urban legends.

However, according to the creators of the website Snopes.com, it seems likely that no matter how thorough they are at researching urban legends, they are unlikely to have much of an impact on how widely and how long they circulate. "People keep falling for the same kind of things over and over again,"[83] says David Mikkelson. His wife, Barbara Mikkelson, agrees, saying that for many people, truth is often much more boring than rumor and legend. "When you're looking at truth versus gossip," she says, "truth doesn't stand a chance."[84]

NOTES

Introduction: What Is an Urban Legend?

1. Maggie Schuler, personal interview with the author, November 19, 2010, St. Paul, MN.
2. Schuler, interview.
3. Schuler, interview.
4. Schuler, interview.
5. Marlys Olson, telephone interview, December 1, 2010.

Chapter 1: "Too Good to Be True"

6. Jan Harold Brunvand, *Too Good to Be True: The Colossal Book of Urban Legends*. New York: Norton, 1999, p. 19.
7. Brunvand, *Too Good to Be True*, p 19.
8. Schuler, interview.
9. Brandon Toropov, *The Complete Idiot's Guide to Urban Legends*. Indianapolis: Alpha, 2001, p. xvii.
10. Berneeta Jacques, telephone interview,

November 14, 2010.

11. Quoted in "Charles R. Drew," WorldLingo, 2011. www.worldlingo.com.
12. Jan Harold Brunvand, *Curses! Broiled Again! The Hottest Urban Legends Going*. New York: Norton, 1989, p. 38.
13. Quoted in Barbara Mikkelson, "The Obstinate Lighthouse," Snopes.com, March 18, 2008. www.snopes.com.
14. Quoted in Harlow Giles Unger, *John Hancock: Merchant King and American Patriot*. New York: Wiley, 2000, p. 241.
15. Clare Pierce, personal interview with the author, December 21, 2010, Minneapolis, MN.
16. Keith Zimmerman and Kent Zimmerman, *Mythbusters: The Explosive Truth Behind 30 of the Most Perplexing Urban Legends of All Time*. New York: Simon Spotlight Entertainment, 2000, p. 150.
17. Quoted in Zimmerman and Zimmerman, *Mythbusters*, p. 154.

18. Pierce, interview.

19. Brunvand, *Too Good to Be True*, p. 26.

Chapter 2: Very Scary

20. Brunvand, *Be Afraid, Be Very Afraid*. New York: Norton, 2004, p. 13.

21. Quoted in Barbara Mikkelson, "Lights Out!," Snopes.com, November 20, 2010. www.snopes.com.

22. Quoted in David Emery, "Flash Your Headlights and Die!," About.com, 2011. http://urbanlegends.about.com.

23. Quoted in Mikkelson, "Lights Out!"

24. "Talking to Us," London Ambulance Service. http://web.archive.org.

25. Quoted in "Pin Prick Attacks," Snopes.com, April 8, 2008. www.snopes.com.

26. N.E. Genge, *Urban Legends: The As-Complete-As-One-Could-Be Guide to Modern Myths*. New York: Three Rivers, 2000, p. 88.

27. Genge, *Urban Legends*, p. 88–89.

28. Quoted in Toropov, *The Complete Idiot's Guide to Urban Legends*, p. 151.

29. Toropov, *The Complete Idiot's Guide to Urban Legends*, p. 151.

30. Quoted in David Emery, "Fear of Licking," About.com, 2011. http://urbanlegends.about.com.

31. Quoted in Barbara Mikkelson and David Mikkelson, "The Accidental Tourist," Snopes.com, August 20, 2007. www.snopes.com.

32. Quoted in Mikkelson and Mikkelson, "The Accidental Tourist."

33. Olson, interview, December 1, 2010.

Chapter 3: Celebrity Urban Legends

34. Genge, *Urban Legends*, p. 186.

35. Quoted in Barbara Mikkelson and David Mikkelson, "Believe It to Beaver," Snopes.com, January 9, 2007. www.snopes.com.

36. Stan Mueller, personal interview with the author, November 29, 2010, Minneapolis, MN.

37. Mueller, interview.

38. Quoted in David Emery, "Was Mr. Rogers a Marine Corps Sniper/Navy Seal?," About.com, 2011. http://urbanlegends.about.com.

39. Quoted in "Memorable Guests Follow-Ups," *Oprah Winfrey Show*, January 1, 2006. www.oprah.com.

40. Quoted in Barbara Mikkelson, "Tommy Rot," Snopes.com, December 1, 2010. www.snopes.com.

41. Quoted in "Memorable Guests Follow-Ups."

42. Quoted in "Memorable Guests Follow-Ups."

43. Quoted in "Memorable Guests Follow-Ups."

44. Quoted in "Ohmigod, Isn't That . . .?," *Cosmopolitan*, October 1997, p. 256.

45. Quoted in Barbara Mikkelson, "Trumped Up," Snopes.com, February 1, 2008. www.snopes.com.

46. Quoted in Mark Milian, "Subway's Jared Fogel's Death Hoaxed," *Los Angeles Times*, June 25, 2008. http://latimesblogs.latimes.com.

47. John Neary, "The Magical McCartney Mystery," *Life*, November 7, 1969, p. 103.

48. Neary, "The Magical McCartney Mystery," p. 104.

49. Quoted in Neary, "The Magical McCartney Mystery," p. 103.

50. Vicky Hennigan, personal interview with the author, November 21, 2010, St. Louis Park, MN.

51. Hennigan, interview.

52. Ronald Heinz, e-mail to the author, January 4, 2011.

53. Quoted in Neary, "The Magical McCartney Mystery," p. 105.

54. Quoted in Neary, "The Magical McCartney Mystery," p. 105.

Chapter 4: Animal Urban Legends

55. Quoted in Brunvand, *Too Good to Be True*, p. 185.

56. Quoted in J.D. Heiman, "Tales from the Urban Crypt," *New York Daily News*, September 13, 1998. www.delorenzosdugout.com.

57. Quoted in Gillian Bennet and Paul Smith, eds., *Urban Legends: A Collection of International Tall Tales and Terrors*. Westport, CT: Greenwood, 2007, p. 152.

58. Marlys Olson, telephone interview, January 4, 2011.

59. Quoted in Bennett and Smith, *Urban Legends*, p. 140.

60. Quoted in Bennett and Smith, *Urban Legends*, p. 140.

61. Quoted in Barbara Mikkelson, "Dinner Party Cat-Astrophe," July 5 2007. www.snopes.com.

62. Quoted in Mikkelson, "Dinner Party Cat-Astrophe."

63. Quoted in Brian T., "Urban Legend—Hercules the World's Biggest Dog," Gather, March 6, 2008. www.gather.com.

64. David Emery, "Hercules, World's Biggest Dog," About.com, 2011. http://

urbanlegends.about.com.

65. Quoted in "Shark Attacks Helicopter!," About.com, 2011. http://urbanlegends. about.com.

66. Stentor Danielson and David Braun, "Shark 'Photo of the Year' Is E-mail Hoax," *National Geographic News*, March 8, 2005. http://news.nationalgeographic. com.

67. Quoted in Barbara Mikkelson and David Mikkelson, "Big Gulp," Snopes.com, June 1, 2010. www.snopes.com.

68. Quoted in Mikkelson and Mikkelson, "Big Gulp."

69. Quoted in Mikkelson and Mikkelson, "Big Gulp."

Chapter 5: Buyer Be Wary!

70. Olson, interview, January 24, 2011.

71. Louise Manning, telephone interview, January 3, 2011.

72. "Double Cheeseburger," McDonald's USA. http://nutrition.mcdonalds.com.

73. David Emery, "Is McDonald's the World's Biggest Purchaser of Cow Eyeballs?," About.com, 2011. http://urbanlegends. about.com.

74. Quoted in David Emery, "The Curse of Frankenchicken," About.com, January 1, 2000. http://urbanlegends.about.com.

75. Quoted in Emery, "The Curse of Frankenchicken."

76. Quoted in "Soda and Pop Rocks," Timeless Myths. www.timelessmyths.co.uk.

77. Quoted in Barbara Mikkelson, "The Biscuit Bullet," Snopes.com, August 16, 2008. www.snopes.com.

78. Quoted in David Emery, "The Neiman Marcus/Mrs. Fields/$250 Cookie Recipe," About.com, 2011. http://urban legends. about.com.

79. Quoted in Emery, "The Neiman Marcus/ Mrs. Fields/$250 Cookie Recipe."

80. Quoted in Emery, "The Neiman Marcus/ Mrs. Fields/$250 Cookie Recipe."

81. Quoted in Emery, "The Neiman Marcus/ Mrs. Fields/$250 Cookie Recipe."

82. Emery, "The Neiman Marcus/Mrs. Fields/ $250 Cookie Recipe."

83. Quoted in Brian Stelter, "Debunkers of Fictions Sift the Net," *New York Times*, April 4, 2010. www.nytimes.com.

84. Quoted in Stelter, "Debunkers of Fictions Sift the Net."

For Further Research

Books

Elizabeth Bardswich, *Urban Legends*. Austin, TX: Steck-Vaughn/Harcourt Achieve, 2006.

Gillian Bennett and Paul Smith, eds., *Urban Legends: A Collection of International Tall Tales and Terrors*. Westport, CT: Greenwood, 2007.

Stuart A. Kallen, *Urban Legends*. Farmington Hills, MI: Lucent, 2006.

Rachel Lynette, *Urban Legends*. Detroit: Kidhaven, 2008.

Richard Roeper, *Debunked! Conspiracy Theories, Urban Legends, and Evil Plots of the 21st Century*. Chicago: Chicago Review, 2008.

Websites

Cokelore, Snopes.com (www.snopes.com/cokelore/cokelore.asp). No beverage has spawned more urban legends in the United States than Coca-Cola. Snopes offers background and links to dozens of them on this site.

Crazy Crittters, About.com (http://urbanlegends.about.com/od/animalkingdom/ig/Crazy-Critters). This site provides photos (many digitally altered) and links to 48 animal urban legends, as well as a few that are actually true. Can you spot them?

Current Hoaxes and Urban Legends (http://urbanlegends.about.com/od/internet/u/current_netlore.htm). This site has links to a variety of individual urban legends, with commentary and analysis to help readers understand how such legends begin.

Death of Little Mikey, Snopes.com (www.snopes.com/horrors/freakish/poprocks.asp). The Snopes fact-checkers take an in-depth look at the beginnings and dissemination of this classic urban legend.

Is Paul Dead? (www.ispauldead.com). With excellent photographs, this site traces the Paul-is-dead urban legends, with an examination of clues from various songs, album covers, and the music itself.

INDEX

PICTURE CREDITS

Cover: iStockphoto.com

ABOUT THE AUTHOR

Gail B. Stewart is the author of more than 280 books for teens and young adults. She lives in Minneapolis, Minnesota. She is married and is the mother of three grown sons.